Wallace & Gromit™
ANORAKNOPHOBIA

Story and Text by
Tristan Davies
Drawings by
Nick Newman

Hodder & Stoughton

By the same authors
WALLACE & GROMIT AND THE LOST SLIPPER

Lettering by Gary Gilbert

Additional colouring by
Tony Trimmer and Fiona Newman

First published in paperback in Great Britain in 1999 by Hodder & Stoughton
A division of Hodder Headline PLC

10 9 8 7 6 5 4 3 2 1

A CIP catalogue record for this title is available from the British Library

ISBN 0 340 72834 5

Printed by Jarrolds Book Printing, Thetford

Hodder & Stoughton
A division of Hodder Headline PLC
338 Euston Road
London
NW1 3BH

Wallace & Gromit™
ANORAKNOPHOBIA

WALLACE
Inventor of the ground- (and furniture) breaking Ping-Pong-O-Matic Automated Home Leisure System who, under hypnosis, learns what it's like to lead a dog's life.

GROMIT
A dog already so busy leading a dog's life (washing the socks, ironing the milk cartons, polishing the Tupperware, etc) he has little time for Home Leisure – even if it is Automated.

MR PATEL
Pigeon fancier and expert on prevailing wind conditions, Wallace's nextdoor neighbour is very interested in, er, wind and pigeons.

DEREK
A game old carrier pigeon and Mr Patel's absolutely favouritest bird.

MR DO IT ALL
Doorman, receptionist, porter, bell boy, gardener and barman at the Hotel Splendio on the Northern Riviera.
(It's a job share.)

THE HERR DOKTOR COUNT BARON NAPOLEON VON STRUDEL, *aka* BERT MAUDSLEY
Dastardly founder of the Acme Corporation and inventor of the Acme Utility Anorak, he has a surprise up his sleeve and something even yukkier behind his eye patch.

THE CONTESSA BARONESS MADAME FRAULEIN QUEENIE VON STRUDEL, *aka* QUEENIE MAUDSLEY
Whip-cracking variety artiste whose arachnid trapeze act has mesmerised audiences from Berlin to Barnoldswick – and sometimes all the way back again.

CLEETHORPES and CLITHEROE
Bert and Queenie's polite, erudite twins, whose hobbies are pressing dried flowers and translating the mystical writings of Thomas à Kempis back into Latin.
OR: Two complete and utter nutters. (Delete where applicable.)

DEREK, DERRICK AND ERIC
Gentleman inventors and exhibitionists, who for the purposes of this story are making an exhibition of themselves at an Acme Corporation-sponsored Invention Convention.

THE SPIDERS FROM MARGATE
A troupe of performing arachnids from Margate and the surrounding area (although one, it's true, was brought up by an aunt in Folkestone).

4

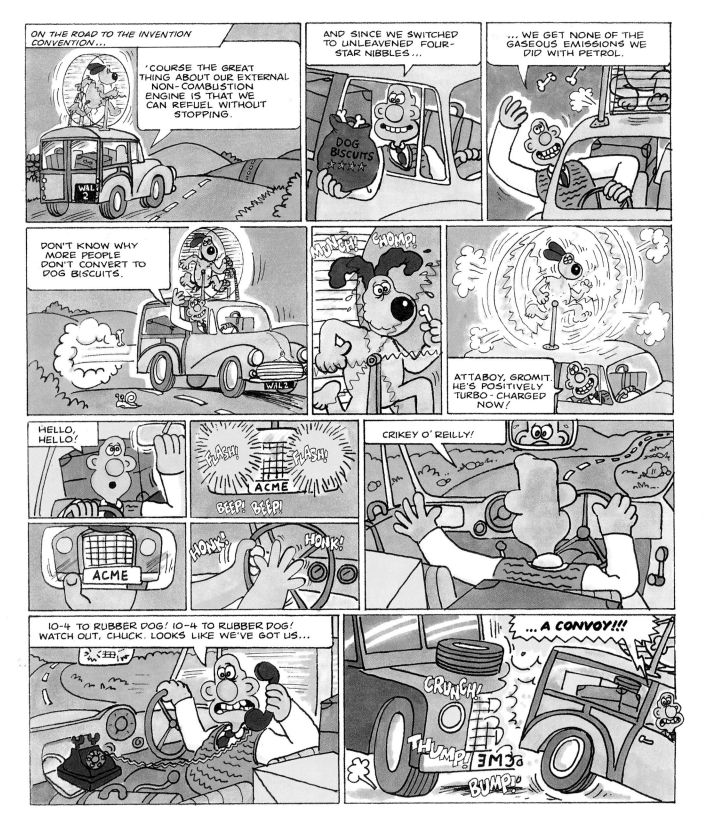

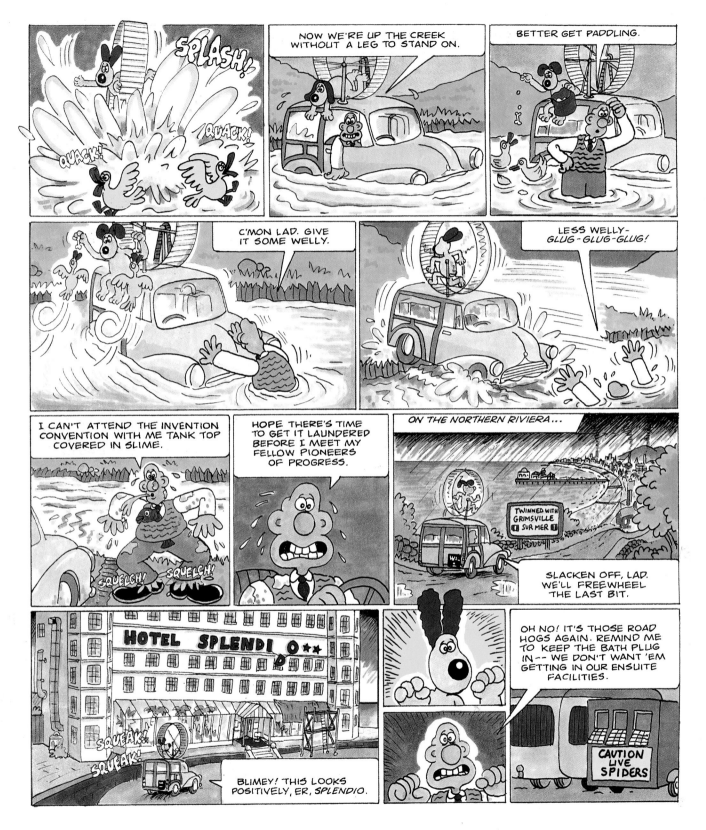

12

14

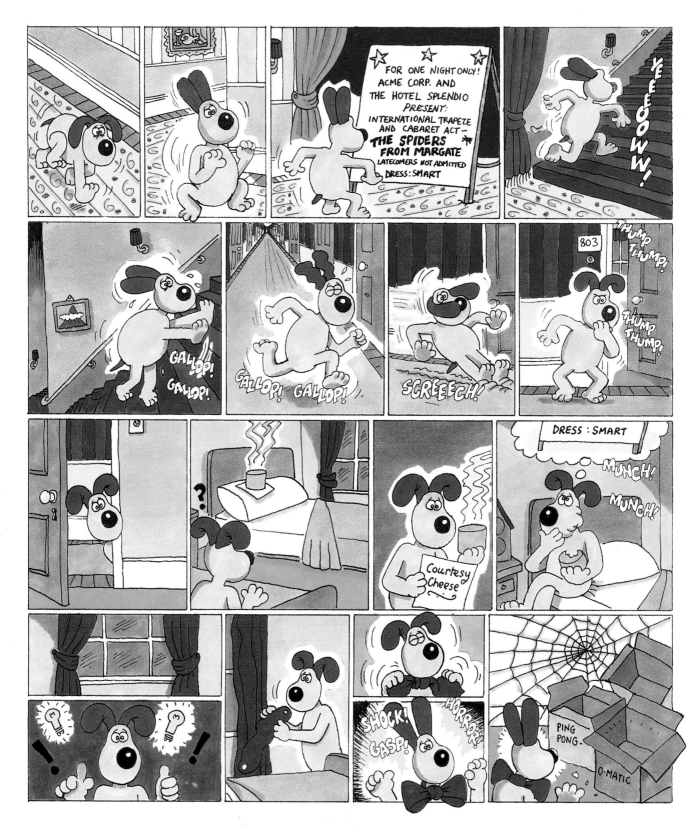

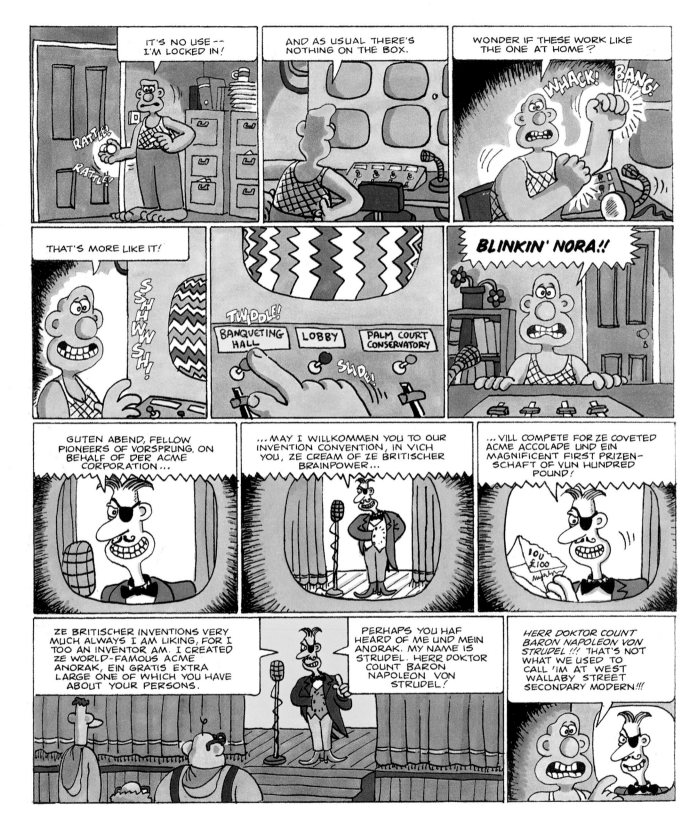

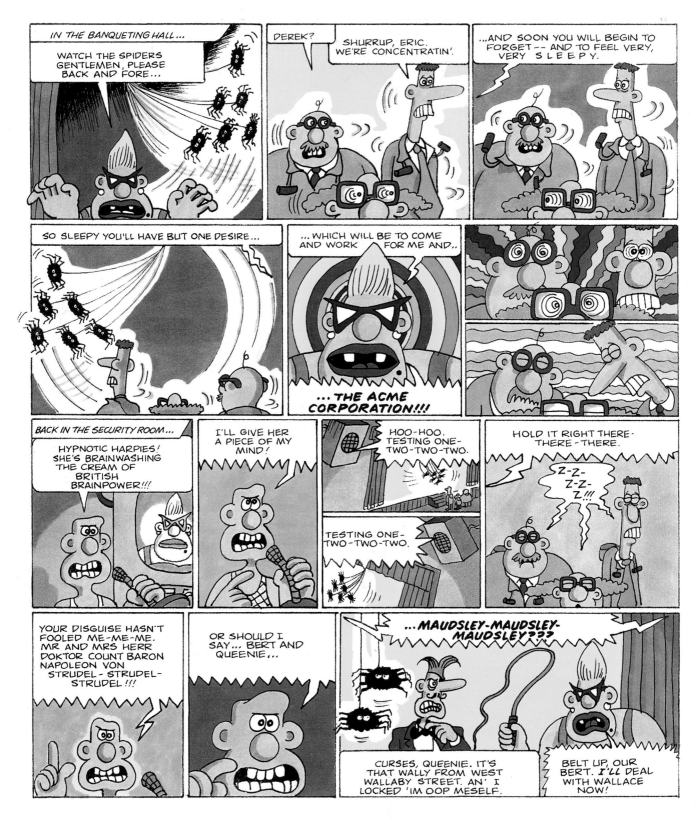

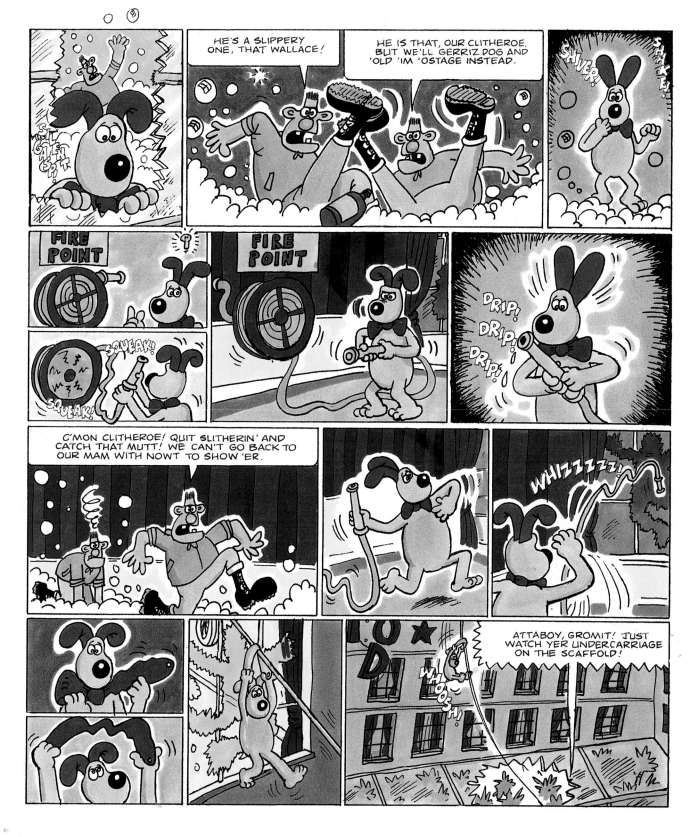

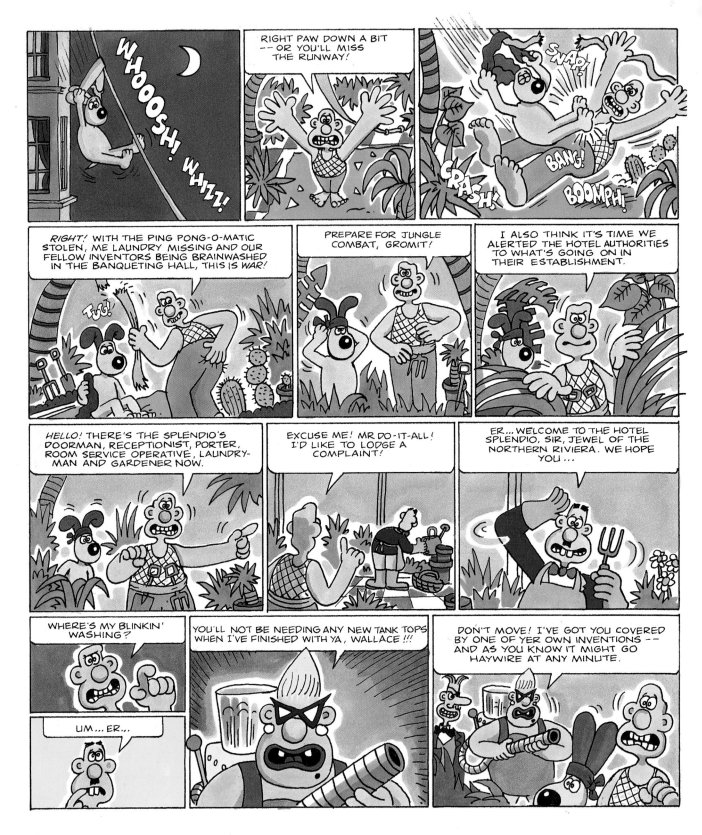

26

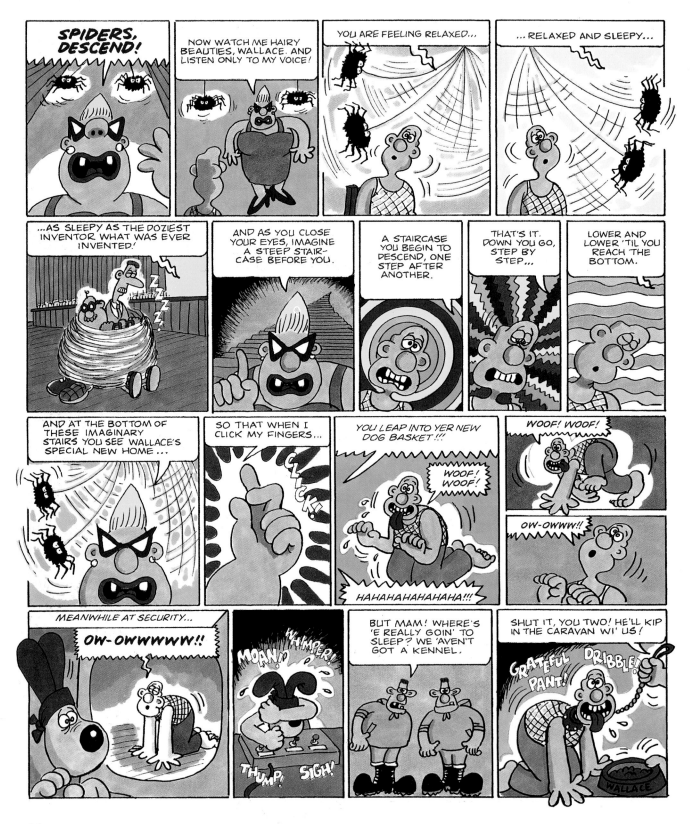

32

33

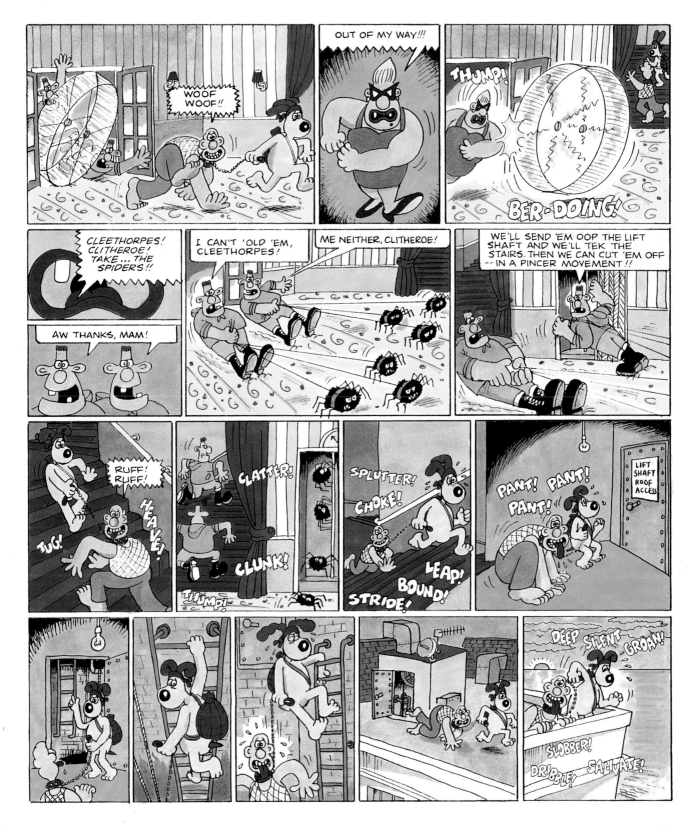

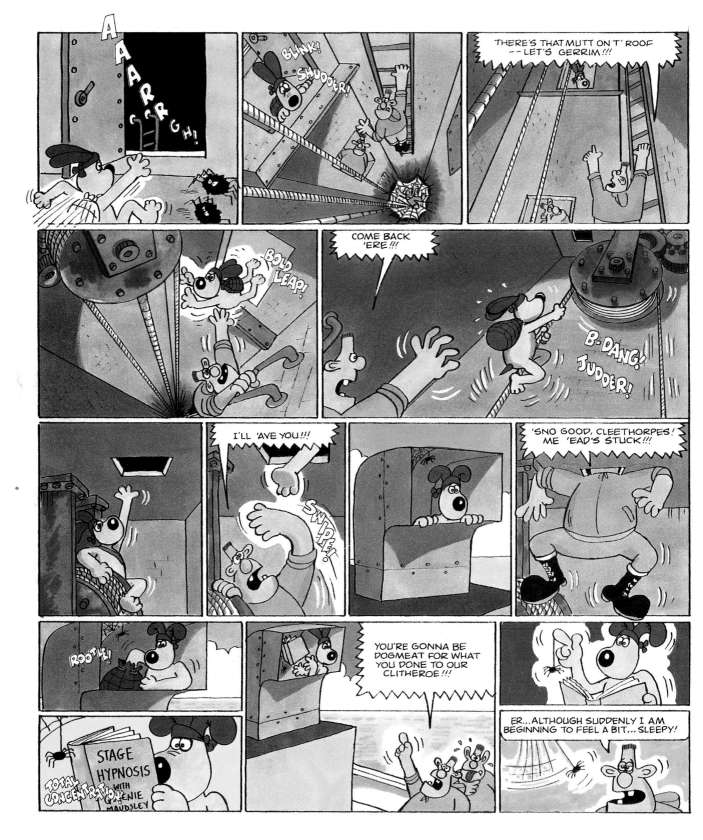

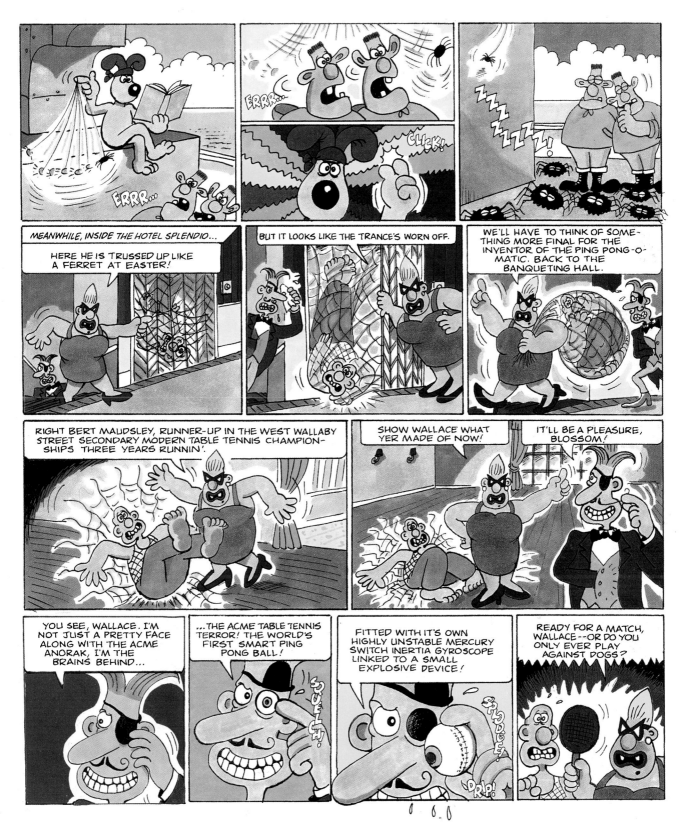

39

40

41